THE

Anne Fine was born and educated in the Midlands and

Also by Anne Fine

Books for Younger Readers

Stranger Danger?
Only a Show
Scaredy-Cat
Design-a-Pram
The Same Old Story Every Year
The Haunting of Pip Parker

Books for Older Readers

Bill's New Frock
The Country Pancake
A Sudden Puff of Glittering Smoke
A Sudden Swirl of Icy Wind
A Sudden Glow of Gold
Anneli the Art Hater
Crummy Mummy and Me
A Pack of Liars
The Angel of Nitshill Road
The Chicken Gave it to Me

ANNE FINE

The Worst Child I Ever Had

Illustrated by Clara Vulliamy

PUFFIN BOOKS

PUFFIN BOOKS

Published by the Penguin Group
Penguin Books Ltd, 27 Wrights Lane, London W8 5TZ, England
Penguin Books USA Inc., 375 Hudson Street, New York, New York 10014, USA
Penguin Books Australia Ltd, Ringwood, Victoria, Australia
Penguin Books Canada Ltd, 10 Alcorn Avenue, Toronto, Ontario, Canada M4V 3B2
Penguin Books (NZ) Ltd, 182–190 Wairau Road, Auckland 10, New Zealand

Penguin Books Ltd, Registered Offices: Harmondsworth, Middlesex, England

First published by Hamish Hamilton 1991
Published in Puffin Books 1993
5 7 9 10 8 6

Filmset in Monophoto Baskerville

Typeset by DatIX International Limited, Bungay, Suffolk
Printed in England by Clays Ltd, St Ives plc

For Mary Benson,
remembering the good times

1.   *Under a Leafy Tree*

Three babysitters sat round the sandpit under a leafy tree.

Mrs Mackle had Mark. He was asleep in his pram, so he was no trouble.

Jeff had the twins, Josh and Jessie. They kept bashing one another with their little wooden spades, and trying to feed each other things they found in the sand – dead insects, bits of grass, old sweetie wrappers – but they weren't much trouble.

Flora had Frances. Frances kept charging off out of sight in the bushes, and Flora had to keep running off to fetch her back. Frances was more trouble than all the other three put together.

"Worst child I ever had," said Jeff, "was a sniffer. Sniffed all the

time. Sniff! Sniff! Sniff! Little
pause, then, *Sniff*! I tell you, this
child nearly drove me mad."

He darted forward to take a
broken end of lolly stick away
from Jessie.

"Worst child I ever had," said
Flora, "was a fusser. Such a
fusser! Fussed if it wasn't the
right cup. Fussed if they weren't
the right gloves. Fussed if you
made the sandwich wrong, or cut
it the wrong way. That child was
a real pain."

She rushed off to fetch Frances
out of the bushes.

Mrs Mackle put out a hand to

rock Mark in his pram while she
waited for Flora to come back.
As soon as Flora was sitting
comfortably on the bench again,
Mrs Mackle said:

"I've babysat for some horrible
children in my time. I had one
who tried to strangle the cat, and
one who screamed if you tried to
make her put on her welly boots.
I've had dozens who wouldn't
go to bed at the right time. And
I've had sneaky ones – children
who are perfectly happy sitting
in your lap reading books and
doing jigsaws, but as soon as they
hear their parents coming home,

they start to wail and howl and act as if you'd spent the evening beating them."

"Now that is sneaky," said Flora, rushing off to fetch Frances.

"Terrible," agreed Jeff, taking a lump of something nasty off Josh.

Mrs Mackle rocked the pram, and waited for Flora to get back. Then she told them:

"But the worst child I ever had lived in one of those houses over there."

She pointed over the park.

"See the red house," she said.

"The one with white windows:
25, Redlands Road. That's
where she lived, the worst child
I ever had."

Overhead, in the tree, a few
leaves stirred.

Mrs Mackle sighed.

"This was a long time ago,"
she said. "Three whole years.
This child was very young then.
She would be older now."

"Tell us about her," said Flora,
running off to fetch Frances.

"Yes, tell us," said Jeff, flicking
a bit of twig out of Jessie's
mouth.

Mrs Mackle rocked the pram

till Flora came back again.
Then:

"It's a horrible story," she
said. "It makes me shiver even
to think about it. You're sure
you want to hear it?"

"Definitely," said Jeff.

"Oh, please!" said Flora.

"All right, then," said Mrs
Mackle. "I'll tell you."

She leaned forward and
whispered so softly that only Flora,
Jeff and the leafy tree could hear.

"Her name was Susan Solly,"
she began.

Up in the tree, young Susan Solly, of 25, Redlands Road, hugged herself happily and smiled.

2. *Snail City*

"She was a pretty little thing,"
said Mrs Mackle. "She was a
peaceful baby. She grew into a
merry toddler, and then into a
cheerful little girl. Everyone

round here loved babysitting for her. She ate all her supper, and cleaned her teeth without making a big fuss, and went to bed when she was told, just like a perfect angel."

"She sounds *wonderful*!" said Flora, rushing off to fetch Frances.

"I wouldn't have minded looking after her," agreed Jeff, taking Jessie's spade away because she was bashing Josh too hard.

"Wait till you *hear*," said Mrs Mackle, darkly.

She rocked the pram till Flora came back again. Then she

carried on.

"Susan Solly liked painting, and doing jigsaws, and watching the telly, and cutting up magazines, and sticking pictures with glue. She liked her woodwork set and she liked helping to cook. But most of all she liked playing in the garden."

Jeff looked over the park towards 25, Redlands Road.

"It's a good garden," he said. "Bushes and grass. Is that an apple tree by the fence?"

"Yes," Mrs Mackle said. "That's where she liked to play. Under the apple tree there is a wheelbarrow upside down in the long grass, next to the compost heap. The family throw all their tea-leaves and apple cores and carrot peelings and shrivelled-up bits of lettuce on to the compost heap. And once a week Susan's mother waters it down with the hose, to make it rot faster."

"Nice place to play!" sniffed Flora.

"Get a bit messy," agreed Jeff.

"She didn't play *in* it," said Mrs Mackle. "Or *on* it. She played beside it, in the long grass. She liked it there because there was an old log, and mossy stones, and lots and lots of snails."

"Snails?"

"*Snails?*"

"Yes, snails," said Mrs Mackle. "Dozens and dozens of them. Snails love damp places, you see. And they love bits of old salad. So you ask your average common-or-garden snail his opinion, and he'll tell you that a mossy stone next to a log beside an upturned wheelbarrow under an apple tree in the long grass close to a compost heap is about the best place in the world to live. Positively palatial!"

"Fancy!" said Flora, rushing off to fetch Frances.

"I didn't realize," said Jeff, wiping something rather peculiar and green off Josh's nose.

"Few people do," said Mrs Mackle. "I never knew much about snails till I babysat for Susan Solly. But she spent hours and hours playing with these snails."

"Playing with them?" said Flora, who had come back.

"Yes," Mrs Mackle said. "Playing. She ran snail parties,

and snail schools, and snail feasts, and snail races. She made snail patterns (though they got restless and they always moved). And if it was dry enough, Susan brought out her paintbox and painted the snails' shells the most beautiful colours in her snail beauty shop."

Mrs Mackle smiled.

"It was a regular snail city, next to that compost heap."

The other two were astonished.

"Didn't she hurt them?" asked Flora.

"Never!" said Mrs Mackle firmly. "Not once. She was as

gentle as I am with a baby." To prove it, she gave Mark a little rock in his pram. "She picked them up carefully and put them back after a very short while. She always let them glide off if they seemed bothered. She wouldn't even run a little zoo in her snail city because she loved them so much she couldn't bear to think of them trapped in anything. No. Fair's fair. You have to give young Susan Solly her due. She was a perfect angel with the snails."

"What was the problem, then?" asked Flora.

"Yes," Jeff agreed. "How did this perfect angel turn out to be the worst child you ever had?"

"Wait till you hear," said Mrs Mackle, darkly.

Up in the leafy tree, Susan Solly smiled.

3. *Doing What She Was Told*

"One day," said Mrs Mackle, "I went off to babysit for Susan Solly. It started to drizzle as I walked up her garden path, and it kept on all morning."

"Nice today, though," said
Flora, rushing off to fetch Frances.

"Better than yesterday,"
agreed Jeff, waiting for Flora to
come back so they could get on
with the story. He spent the time
shaking some of the sand out of
Jessie's nappy.

Flora rushed back and sat
down.

"Go on," she said to Mrs
Mackle.

Mrs Mackle went on.

"Susan, of course, had gone
out to play with the snails. I could
see her through the window.
First she fixed up a snail snack,

offering them some juicy fresh titbits she found on the very top of the compost heap. Then she organized a Great Snail Expedition through the wet grass and over the mossy boulders. I think they were supposed to be heading for the rosebush, but a lot of them kept straying."

"It must have been a very slow expedition," said Jeff.

"It certainly was. And while it was taking place, the drizzle turned into raindrops, and the raindrops turned into a downpour. Susan was in her raincoat and hat and boots, but by the middle of the morning, she looked soaking wet."

"I would have called her inside," said Flora, rushing off to fetch Frances.

"So would I," agreed Jeff, rescuing a ladybird Josh was trying to pat with his spade.

"I tried," said Mrs Mackle. "I did try. I opened the window and leaned out.

'You'd better come in now, Susan,' I told her.

'Susan, did you hear me?' I asked.

'I don't want to have to tell you again, dear,' I said.

'Come in and we'll watch

cartoons. *Snail Show* is on telly
next and you know it's your
favourite,' I wheedled.

'If you don't come in, I shall
have to tell your mother,' I
threatened.

'Susan! Come in right now!'
I ordered.

'*Susan!*' I yelled.

'If you don't come in right this minute, I shall come out there and *drag* you in,' I shrieked.

'SUSAN!!! GET IN THIS HOUSE RIGHT NOW!' I bellowed. And I slammed the

window shut so hard I broke a pane."

The other two stared. Jeff's mouth had dropped open. Flora looked aghast.

Jeff said, "What happened?"

Mrs Mackle said, "Would you believe it, after all that time pretending she had cloth ears, that cheeky little madam suddenly gave a secret little smile, whispered something to the snails, then stood up and walked, calm as you please, towards the house."

"Doing what she was told at last!" said Flora. (She sounded

quite relieved.)

"Wait till you hear," warned Mrs Mackle darkly.

Up in the tree, young Susan Solly gave yet another little secret smile, and hugged herself again.

4. *Snail Show*

Flora rushed off to fetch Frances.
When she came back, she said to
Mrs Mackle, "I don't think I
would have sat and watched
Snail Show cartoons with Susan

Solly after all that."

"Neither would I," agreed Jeff, prising Josh and Jessie apart because they were trying to bite one another. "I'd have been far too cross."

"I was, too," said Mrs Mackle. "I went straight into the kitchen to make myself a cup of coffee. I didn't even offer Susan orange juice. And she didn't come in and ask for it. She just kept marching back and forth from her toy cupboard under the stairs to the front room, carrying armfuls of tiny plastic chairs from her doll's house.'

"A nice change," said Flora. "Playing with stuff from her doll's house."

Mrs Mackle snorted.

"Wait till you hear," Jeff warned Flora, to save Mrs Mackle the bother of saying it darkly. Then he turned to Mrs Mackle. "Carry on."

She carried on.

"I sat at the table in the kitchen, sipping my coffee and nibbling a nice digestive biscuit. After a while, I heard Susan switch on the television in the front room."

"Was it *Snail Show* cartoons?"

asked Flora, as she rushed off to fetch Frances.

"Yes," Mrs Mackle told her when she came back. "I recognized the silly song they always sing."

"And did Susan sit and watch it all by herself?" asked Jeff, prising Josh and Jessie apart because they were trying to poke one another's eyes out.

"I thought she did," said Mrs Mackle. "That's what I thought at first. But then, in between sips of coffee and nibbles of biscuit, I thought I heard the back door quietly open. And quietly close.

And open. And close. And open.
And close."

"How strange . . ." said Flora.

"Very odd . . ." agreed Jeff.

"Just what I thought," said
Mrs Mackle. "So I called out,
'Susan, are you all right, dear?'
And she called back, 'Yes, thank
you, Mrs Mackle'."

"She sounds like a perfect
angel," Jeff said wistfully, prising
Josh and Jessie apart because
they were trying to pull one
another's hair out.

"Wait till you hear," warned
Flora, to save Mrs Mackle the
bother of saying it darkly. Then

she rushed off to fetch Frances.

When she came back, Mrs Mackle took up the tale.

"So I drank up my coffee and finished my biscuit. And just as I was rinsing the cup under the tap, I thought I heard the back door again. Open. And close."

"Weird . . ." Flora said.

"Most peculiar . . ." agreed Jeff.

"So I thought I'd better go and take a look."

"You never know," said Flora.

"Better safe than sorry," agreed Jeff.

"I walked across the kitchen

and opened the door. There was nothing in the hall, just the door of the toy cupboard under the stairs swinging open, and Susan's doll's house empty on the floor."

Flora looked round for Frances. But, tired suddenly from all that running away into the bushes, Frances had climbed quietly into her pushchair, and fallen fast asleep.

Jeff glanced in the sandpit. Josh was squashed up as close to Jessie as he could get, sucking his own thumb but patting Jessie's chubby thigh. Jessie's eyes were drooping.

"Go on," whispered Flora.

"Yes, go on," whispered Jeff.

"I walked down the hall and pushed open the door of the front room. At first I saw nothing special – just the same old furniture in the same old places,

and, on the television, *Snail Show*
cartoons blaring away."

"To an empty room?"

"Nobody watching?"

"That's what I thought at
first! But then I saw!"

Mrs Mackle's face drained
dead white at the memory. Up

in the branches overhead, a few leaves stirred as if a breeze had rippled through the tree.

"Saw *who*?" whispered Flora.

"Saw *what*?" whispered Jeff.

Mrs Mackle leaped to her feet, tearing her hair at the memory.

"Dozens of them!" she cried. "Dozens of the horrible, slimy, slithery things! Each one perched on its own tiny plastic doll's chair! Each one with its little head poked out of its shell, and its little horns straining! A whole lot of them, looking for all the world as if they were at a little private cinema, watching a show on the big screen!"

"*Snail Show!*"

"*Snail Show!*"

"It was horrible!" cried Mrs Mackle. "Horrible! Horrible! It was the worst sight that I have ever seen in all my years of babysitting. And if I live to be a hundred years old, Susan Solly will always be the worst child I ever had!"

"There, there," soothed Flora. "Try and calm yourself. It's all over now."

"That's right," agreed Jeff. "You said yourself, all this happened a long time ago."

He put his arms around the shaking Mrs Mackle as the leaves of the tree overhead rustled gently and, six feet above him, Susan Solly smiled.

"Time to go home," Jeff said. "This afternoon seems to have gone very fast. It's almost tea time."

Pulling her coat around her shoulders, Mrs Mackle slipped

the brake off the pram.

"See you tomorrow," she said, and set off for the north gate.

"Cheerio," said Flora, wheeling the pushchair towards the west gate.

Jeff strapped the twins into the double buggy.

"Bye!" he called over his shoulder as he hurried off to the east gate.

There was a moment's silence. Then, with a rustle of leaves, young Susan Solly slid easily down the tree trunk and set off, calm as you please, across the

park to the south gate and 25,
Redlands Road.

She was still smiling.

Also in Young Puffin

PUGWASH
AND THE MIDNIGHT FEAST

PUGWASH
AND THE WRECKERS

John Ryan

"Havin' a midnight feast, eh?" roared Jake, "and never thought of askin' *us* to join you?"

Captain Pugwash and his crew are interrupted eating their midnight feast by some very unwelcome visitors – Cut-throat Jake and his bloodthirsty buccaneers! The greedy villains take over, but not for long...And there's more crafty plotting from the evil Jake when he sets out to wreck the *Black Pig*, full of the biggest load of bullion ever!

PUGWASH
AND THE MUTINY

PUGWASH
AND THE FANCY-DRESS PARTY

John Ryan

Two hilarious tales starring that most amiable of pirates, Captain Pugwash!

It's mutiny on board the *Black Pig,* but when Captain Pugwash and his cabin boy Tom are cast ashore, things don't quite work out as the mutinous crew have planned, for the dastardly Cut-throat Jake and his bloodthirsty band make an unexpected entrance! And the same villain is out to spoil Pugwash's devious plan for a fancy-dress ball, which would have filled his chests with treasure!

Also in Young Puffin

The Strawberry-Jam Pony

Sheila Lavelle

"The ponies, Dad! What will happen to the ponies?"

It's Tommy Wilson's greatest dream to be able to work alongside his brother with the pit ponies. But he's got another five years to wait until he's old enough to go down the mine. Then the miners come out on strike and Tommy's help is needed to bring the ponies up to the surface. His favourite is Gleam, the pony who loves to eat strawberry-jam sandwiches – and with Gleam, Tommy's adventures *really* begin!

Also in Young Puffin

ONE NIL

Tony Bradman

Dave Brown is football mad!

All Dave ever thinks about is football,
even in the classroom. He just can't
concentrate on anything else! So imagine
Dave's excitement when he finds out the
England squad are coming to train at his
local club! He desperately wants to go
and see them – but what about school?
At first it seems impossible, but then
Dave works out an ingenious plan – a
plan that leads him to scoring the goal of
a lifetime!

Also in Young Puffin

Ninety-nine Dragons

Barbara Sleigh

"I think sheep are soppy," said Ben scornfully.

Beth and Ben's father suggested counting sheep jumping over a gate, to help them go to sleep. But Ben thought dragons would be much more interesting than ordinary old sheep, so he sent *them* jumping over the gate instead! What he hadn't intended, though, was for his ninety-nine greedy green dragons to jump into the same field as Beth's fifty sweet little sheep!

SEE YOU AT THE MATCH

Margaret Joy

"It's a goal!"

The six stories in this collection are all about young football fans who watch or play the game that makes them so happy...or sad! Experience with them the excitement of your first match and the thrill of scoring the winning goal, as well as the disappointment when your team loses or you miss the big match.

HELP!

Margaret Gordon

"Help! Help! Help!"

Fred and Flo are very helpful little pigs.
The problem is, the more helpful they try
to be, the more trouble they cause.
Whether they are washing Grandad's car,
looking after Baby or doing the
decorating, disaster is never far away.